To my Dream Maker,
1st Lt. Jack R. Money
U.S. Air Corps
1922 - 1944

Once, a long time ago, a little girl named Flavia lived in an old wooden house . . . with funny old chairs on the porch.

Flavia lived with her younger brother, Willie, who always wore a belt and suspenders, socks that scrunched down in his shoes . . . and pants that were too short.

They lived with Mama, who danced
to the music on the radio . . . and
knew how to make cloth dolls
that looked like people.

Flavia thought Mama was
a dancing angel sent
from Heaven.

She liked thinking that.

And they lived with Grandma, whom they called Mammo. She planted geraniums in coffee cans, and grew sweet potato vines in jars . . . and always wore an apron.

And with Flavia's uncle, Jack, who wore a rose-colored scarf, was a magical storyteller . . . and knew how to make people smile.

Flavia thought of Jack as her big brother. She liked thinking that.

Flavia was her real name, and she wished she could change it. It was funny sounding and she always had to spell and pronounce it slowly: FLA-VI-A. She was different looking, tall and skinny, with dark hair and green eyes. She wished she could change and look just like her friends.

Especially she wished she could change where she lived.

Their house was rickety and had those funny old chairs on the porch. It was by the side of an alley and across the street from a tire factory. She was afraid she would live there forever, and wished and wished she lived somewhere else.

TIRE
COMPANY

On Sundays, aunts and uncles and cousins would come to see Mammo. Everyone was happy to be together, and they would wave hello and goodbye and they hugged each other.

Sometimes Flavia, Willie and Jack would put on a show. They would dress up as clowns and do cartwheels and almost always Flavia would tap dance.

As a finale, Jack would reach into a magic bag and pretend he had wonderful dreams for everyone. Flavia liked that part the best.

After dinner, the whole family would sit around the fig tree in the yard and in the funny old chairs from the porch. They would talk and tell stories and sing songs until it got dark.

Flavia and Willie always thought Mama sang the best . . . but of course she did, she was an angel. Mama's songs told stories about people afraid to say "I love you," and afraid to take a chance.

The words always made Flavia cry. Mama said they were songs her Papa had taught her that his mother had taught him . . . which made Flavia think maybe they had been angels too. She liked thinking that.

On Tuesdays, everyone on Flavia's street gave anything they didn't want or couldn't fix to The Hanky Man who would drive his truck down the alley by the side of the house. Mammo would always try to have something ready for Flavia and Willie to give him, but broken things weren't easy to find in their house because Mama could fix anything.

The Hanky Man's truck was piled high with worn-out furniture and ragged clothes and toys and lamps and clocks and violins and papers and bottles.

He wore a hat and suspenders and had a bandana around his neck. He spoke with an accent and when he wasn't playing a harmonica, he was singing. Flavia didn't understand the words to his songs and she had thought for a long time maybe he was a gypsy. She liked thinking that.

Flavia was afraid to tell her friends about The Hanky Man. She was afraid they would laugh and not believe he was real.

They'd probably never seen anyone like him because none of them lived in a house across the street from a tire factory, by the side of an alley.

Sometimes at night before she went to sleep, and when everything was quiet except for the crickets, Flavia would look up at the moon and the stars and make wishes.

She thought the moon was a light in the night sky and that Heaven was just on the other side.

She would tell the moon things she was afraid to say to anyone, especially Mama. She loved Mama so much she never wanted to hurt her feelings, but she had to tell someone how she felt inside, so she talked to the moon.

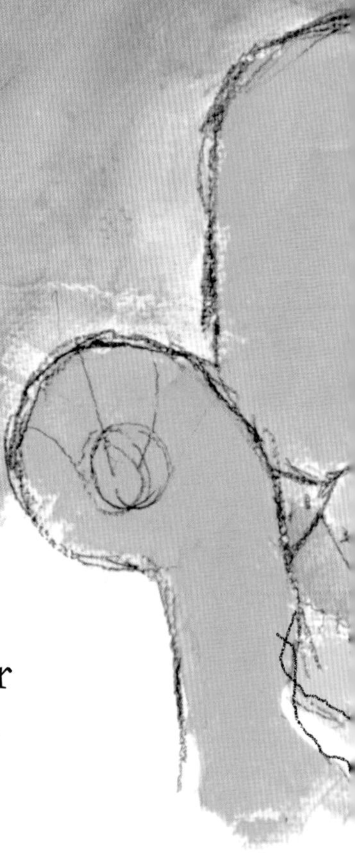

She told him how much she wished she could change her name and the way she looked, and how much she wanted to move away from where she lived. For a long time, she wondered if he ever heard her.

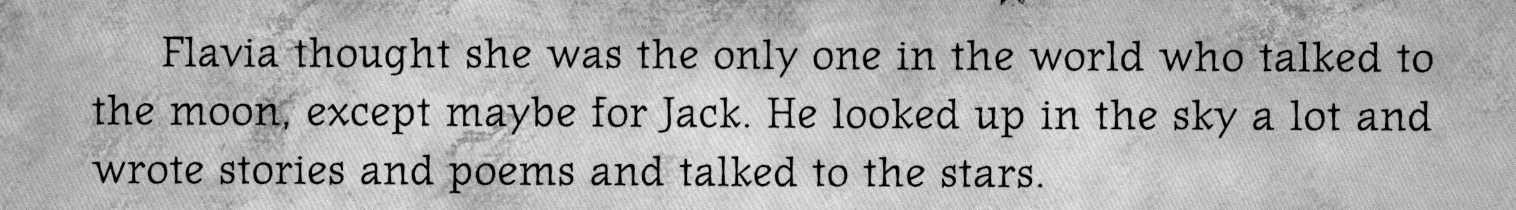

Flavia thought she was the only one in the world who talked to the moon, except maybe for Jack. He looked up in the sky a lot and wrote stories and poems and talked to the stars.

He loved being alive, and he danced and sang as though wonder and surprises were all around him . . . and as though he had a thousand dreams.

Flavia knew there was something special about him, like maybe he had a secret. She liked thinking that.

She had always wanted to tell Jack how much she loved him and how important he was to her life . . .

and how when she was around him she felt some of his wonder rub off on her.

But she was afraid to say it, so she kept it inside . . . and the words just wouldn't come.

For a long time, she wondered if he ever knew.

One Saturday, Jack was sitting in the yard under the fig tree. "Come sit beside me, Flavia," he said. "I've something to give you." Then, reaching into his magic bag, he gave her a handful of paper stars.

He put his arm around her and said softly, "I hear you crying sometimes at night as you look up at the moon. I know there are many things you wish to change, so listen carefully, there's something I want you to know.

"The moon shines down on all of us from his place in the sky. He shines on you and me, your friends and The Hanky Man . . . on all people, and on all the world. He hears every wish you ever wished and wants you to be happy."

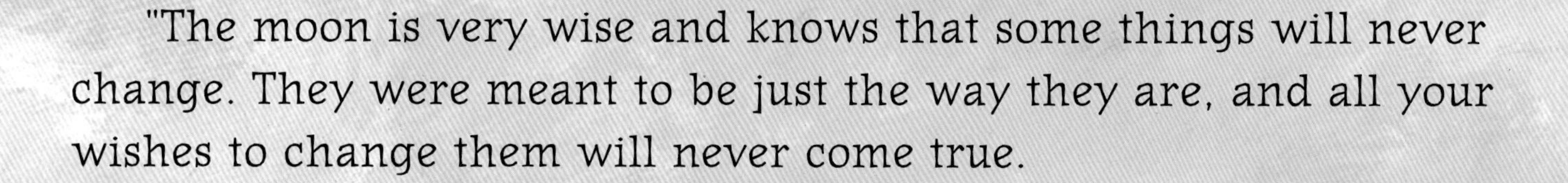

"The moon is very wise and knows that some things will never change. They were meant to be just the way they are, and all your wishes to change them will never come true.

"But he wants you to know you can dream, and if you believe and are not afraid to reach high, work hard and never give up, you can make those dreams come true.

"The only thing that needs to change is the way you feel inside, and only you can change that. Once you know this . . . it's a wonderful feeling."

"One of your wishes was to change your name. But your Mama named you after a princess in a book she read a long time ago.

"She loved you so much, she kept that name in her heart for you until you were born. It's a beautiful name."

"You wished you looked like your friends, but you have your Mama's dark hair and green eyes, and you are tall and thin like your Daddy.

"You are beautiful because you are a part of your parents and your grandparents, and pieces of all their dreams," Jack said.

"These are the things you can never change, for they are the precious things that make you you. That's why you are important and that's why you matter.

"I heard you tell the moon you wished you didn't live in this old wooden house," Jack continued, "but there is much in life to love no matter where we live.

"And this house is special because it is our house, the place we can all be together . . . the place where we can all be real."

"We've worked and laughed and cried in this house. You've made wishes and even talked to the moon from its windows.

"You've sat on those steps and listened to your Mama sing. Mammo has sat on those funny old chairs on the porch and watched you dance.

"We've shared all the little things a family shares, but mostly we've shared love, and this is what you'll remember because love never leaves us . . . it's what we take with us wherever we go. How lucky we are to live together in this old wooden house."

"You are ashamed you live by the side of an alley, but on Tuesdays that alley brings you a beautiful parade with The Hanky Man, his music and magic, and ribbons of color . . . all the things that make us smile."

"When we give some of our things to him, then those things become a part of the parade and make other people smile because there is still beauty in broken things if they've been loved," Jack said.

"Once you understand this . . . it's a wonderful feeling."

"I've watched you and Willie play around this fig tree. I've sat under it, written my stories and left it filled with my dreams."

"Now it's your time, your dreams are on their way.
It's become your tree and your place to dream."

"When you climb it, let your dreams reach high enough and they will take you to the sky. You will see above the tire factory and over the clouds and into your tomorrows.

"You were put on this earth to be a part of everything you see. It is your life, and you can go anywhere, be anything and do anything you dream of."

Jack got up, looked at her and said, "Promise me, Flavia, that when you grow up you will never stop dreaming.

"And that if one dream should fall and break into a thousand pieces, never be afraid to pick up one of those pieces and begin again.

"Each piece can be a new dream to believe in and to reach for. This is life's way of touching you and giving you strength.

"Remember that dreams are free like the moon in the sky and the stars in your hands, and those who know how to dream will walk in stardust. Once you understand this . . . it's a wonderful feeling."

Flavia looked at the paper stars she held in her hands and thought for a long time about what Jack had said.

Now she was proud of her name and knew that with her dark hair and green eyes, she would always be a part of Mama and Daddy.

And she knew that all the people who lived in this old wooden house loved her, and this was special and what really mattered. How lucky she was to know this.

Why, at night, the moon even shined on the tire factory . . .

. . . and a musical parade was hers as it came down her very own alley every Tuesday.

The fig tree would be her place now, her place to dream. Flavia knew that when she grew up there'd be other places, because it didn't really matter where you dreamed . . . only that you dreamed.

So she called to her little brother. "Willie," she said, "come sit beside me, I've something to give you." And gently putting her arm around him . . . she gave him a handful of paper stars.

Then Flavia watched Jack as he slowly walked away, and the words came easily to her now. "I love you, Jack," she said softly.

He was looking up into the sky and she knew he was dreaming that someday he would be a flyer and touch those clouds and maybe even the moon.

The paper stars Jack carried in his magic bag had spilled and were scattering around his lavender shoes where he walked. They were shining now, just like stardust.

Now Flavia understood the wonder of Jack, and how he always made people around him feel better inside.

He was wise like the moon, and he did have a secret. He was a Dream Maker. Flavia understood it all now . . . and it was a wonderful feeling.

Years passed . . .

Now, sometimes when looking up at the moon,
Flavia is sure she can see the faint image
of a rose-colored scarf
and the glimmer of lavender shoes.

She often smiles and thinks
maybe Jack is the real man in the moon.

She likes thinking that.